Joseph Lyman

A Sermon Preached Before His Excellency James Bowdoin

Joseph Lyman

A Sermon Preached Before His Excellency James Bowdoin

ISBN/EAN: 9783337405496

Printed in Europe, USA, Canada, Australia, Japan

Cover: Foto ©Andreas Hilbeck / pixelio.de

More available books at **www.hansebooks.com**

A
SERMON,

PREACHED BEFORE

His Excellency JAMES BOWDOIN, Esq.

GOVERNOUR;

His Honour THOMAS CUSHING, Esq.

LIEUTENANT-GOVERNOUR;

The Honourable the
COUNCIL, and the Honourable the
SENATE, and HOUSE of
REPRESENTATIVES,

Of the COMMONWEALTH of

MASSACHUSETTS,

May 30, 1787.

BEING THE DAY OF

GENERAL ELECTION.

By Rev. JOSEPH LYMAN,
PASTOR of the CHURCH in HATFIELD.

BOSTON:
PRINTED by ADAMS and NOURSE,
Printers to the Honourable the GENERAL COURT.

AN

Election SERMON.

ROMANS, CHAP. XIII. VERSE 4, firſt clauſe.

For he is the Miniſter of GOD *to thee for good.*

IT is the appropriate privilege of chriſtianity, to afford doctrines and precepts adapted to the circumſtances of all characters of men. Other ſyſtems of morality are partial in their inſtructions, deficient in motives, and erroneous in the maxims of human life. But the author of our faith hath grounded our obligations upon a rational foundation, excited us to duty by ſuitable and efficient motives, and extended his inſtructions to every claſs of men. With equal regards he reſpects the wiſe and the noble, the uninſtructed and him of low degree. To render his ſyſtem the more beneficial, he has appointed miniſters to explain its principles, and inculcate his ſaving doctrines upon men of all degrees ; to vindicate and magnify his inſtitutions before Kings, and to preach the goſpel to the poor.

AND

AND this is the minifter's happinefs, that he is ready furnifhed with inftructions fuited to every auditory before whom he may fpeak. All men need inftruction, to be prompted to the difcharge of their fupreme obligations to God, and their relative obligations to each other. And this is their common privilege, that the bleffed Jefus, by his written word and preached gofpel, provides for all *a portion in due feafon.*

THE words felected for the bafis of a difcourfe upon the prefent occafion, contain inftruction for rulers ; to point them to the origin of their power and the ufe they fhould make of it : They comprize a leffon equally ufeful to fubjects ; how to conduct themfelves in relation to their rulers, and what views to entertain of their authority.

SHOULD the Preacher conform himfelf to the text, and place to view the folemn importance of it, the prefent occafion might be richly profitable to this great affembly. May that Divine Teacher, *who fpake as never man fpake,* by the aids of his Spirit, affift the Preacher *to find out acceptable words and the words of truth and fobernefs* ; to recommend his doctrines in their purity and power to his fervants, now convened to learn the law in his fanctuary.

For

For he is the minister of God to thee for good.

Our first enquiry is, Who is this minister of God? The context informs us, that *he is the civil magistrate,* called in a preceding passage, *the higher powers,* since the magistrate is raised in the community to a station above his brethren, and intrusted with authority to govern others, by ordaining and executing laws for the common good. That magistrates are designated by the Apostle, appears from his terming them, *Rulers who are not a terror to good works, but to the evil* ; they are appointed to support good morals and punish vice. And this part of the description agrees with the civil magistrate, *He is a revenger to execute wrath upon him that doth evil :* And as an acknowledgement of his services and dignity, *he receives tribute.* It is thus evident from the Apostle's calling him *the Higher Powers, the Ruler and the Revenger,* that the *civil magistrate* is intended by *the minister of God.* In speaking upon this subject, four general propositions will merit our attention, viz.

I. That civil authority is of divine institution.

II. That civil authority is instituted for the good of the people in general, and for the benefit of the church of Christ in particular.

III. What measures must the civil authority pursue to answer the end of their institution?

IV.

IV. What are the obligations of subjects to the civil authority?

1. Civil authority is of Divine institution.

He is the minister of God.

Order is Heaven's first law. Without it the gracious designs of the Creator cannot be accomplished. He has made his creatures of various powers and degrees ; rising by an easy and happy gradation, from the lowest species of animals, to the most exalted rank of heavenly intelligencies. Creatures of the same species are constituted with certain differences, by which they greatly excel each other. Men, who are said to be born in a state of equality, are yet endowed with unequal measures of strength and wisdom. And hence there is a greater variety amongst men, than amongst several different species of animals. Some are qualified to teach and guide ; others to be taught and led by their superiors. To affirm that in the qualifications to rule and guide, all men are equal, is to blend characters totally diverse, to confound wisdom with folly, and affability and condescension with ill-nature and pride. There have ever been distinctions in the world, and various degrees amongst men ; while endowed
with

with such various qualities and affections, the distinction will remain. To gainsay this distinction, is to counteract one of the principal laws of humanity. Some must be in authority; others in subordination. And happy is that people who are allowed in Providence, to look out from among their brethren persons of the best disposition, and most aptly qualified to rule over them.

THAT particular persons should be distinguished and exalted in society, may be argued from the methods of Providence, ever since man hath been upon earth. No people were ever able to subsist for any length of time, without forming into some kind of civil government, and setting aside those boasted equalities, with which men are born into the world. They must be subject to some common rule and authority, in order to possess any measure of happiness and security. Where there are no rulers to govern the community, all things are immediately involved in confusion and misery. The continuance of our original equality, is a state of nature, and all ages have found a state of nature to be a state of war. Therefore it has pleased the common Parent of men, to lead them to a state of civil subordination, by which a part of the community are intrusted to ordain and carry into effect, laws and regulations for the whole.　　B　:　　THAT

THAT the eftablifhment of civil government is by the counfel and wifdom of God, we are taught both from the hiftory of his Providence, and the teftimony of his infpired truth. Ifrael, the people of his love, were formed into a civil community, and made fubordinate to eftablifhed laws, to be adminiftered by rulers appointed for that purpofe. And it was a time of fore rebuke, when there was no magiftrate in the land of fufficient authority, to put them in fear. The exaltation and degradation of rulers is the work of God, and not the pro- duction of a blind and fortuitous chance, accord- ing to the opinion of idle and infidel wits. *For* faith the word of enlightning truth, * *Promotion cometh neither from the eaft, nor from the weft, nor from the fouth. But God is the Judge ; he putteth down one and fetteth up another.* The prerogative of or- daining magiftracy and civil authority, belongs to our Lord Jefus Chrift ; this claim he affumes to himfelf under the name of Wifdom.† " *By me Kings reign and Princes decree juftice. By me Princes rule, and nobles, even all the judges of the earth.*" Thefe words imply the power of God, in fupporting civil authority, and alfo his approbation of civil magiftracy,

* Pfalm, lxxv. 6, 7.
† Prov. viii. 15, 16.

magiſtracy, as one of the bleſſings of the Redeemer's purchaſe. In what eſtimation the bleſſing of civil government is holden by God, may be learned from that apoſtolical direction to Titus, how to teach the flock of Chriſt. * " *Put them in mind to be ſubject to principalities and powers, and to obey magiſtrates.*" So far is Chriſt intereſted in the ſupport of civil authority, that he will acknowledge thoſe only to be his followers, who willingly obey rulers, and ſubmit to their adminiſtrations.

But we need not go far for arguments : Our text is encompaſſed with proofs of the Divine inſtitution of civil authority. The argument in the firſt verſe, for ſubjection to the *higher powers*, is, *For there is no power, but of God : the powers that be, are ordained of God.* The reaſon alledged for not oppoſing *the power*, is in the ſecond verſe. *Whoſoever reſiſteth the power, reſiſteth the ordinance of God : and they that reſiſt ſhall receive to themſelves damnation.* Thrice in this argument the Apoſtle ſtiles the magiſtrate, *God's miniſter* ; that is, a public ſervant appointed by God. He is ſtiled alſo God's *revenger to execute wrath upon him that doth evil.* And Chriſtians muſt needs be ſubject, not only from fear and conſtraint, but chearfully in diſcharge of

a

* Titus, iii. 1.

a good conscience. Therefore our argument for the Divine institution of civil authority, rests upon the uniformity of Providence, in bringing mankind under government ; upon the clear testimony of scripture ; and upon our Lord's repeated instructions to his disciples to yield a willing homage to rulers, even when they are neither of their faith, nor even of exemplary morals.

Not that God hath ordained any particular form of Government. This is left to the judgement of men, and the circumstances of particular countries and communities. But some government is necessary. God wills mankind to be in subordination, and that they stand to each other in the relation of rulers and subjects. He does not set up the claim of Kings, to an indefeasible and hereditary right : Such a claim is without support in scripture, and is repugnant to common sense. The leading idea of scripture is, That communities constitute certain of their brethren to rule over them : and thus constituted, they are the *ordinance* of the Supreme Ruler.

Our argument is not, That every power which assumes to be authority is really so ; or that God would have it acknowledged as his institution.

Usurpers

Ufurpers and incurable tyrants are not the ordinance of God. Invaders are to be rejected as hoftile to civil authority and fubverfive of government. The Apoftle would fhow, That rulers allowed by long ufe, fubmitted to by promifes of allegiance, or introduced according to the ftated maxims of the community over whom they prefide, are invefted with power by God himfelf, and are to be obeyed by Chriftians as his ordinance; and this, however their characters may be faulty, and their adminiftrations in many refpects injudicious and reprehenfible.

I proceed to prove,

II. THAT civil authority is inftituted for the good of the people in general, and for the benefit of the church of Chrift in particular.

He is the Minifter of God to THEE *for* GOOD.

THAT God has inftituted civil authority for the common good, is a full demonftration, that he utterly abhors that tyranny and oppreffion, which is fo frequently practifed by the infolent Rulers of the earth : His benevolence is incenfed at the abufe of his gifts, and the perverfion of thofe powers and talents which he has beftowed upon magiftrates for the happinefs of his creatures. Rulers, who mifapply their authority for their
personal

perfonal advantage, and ufe the force of the State, to feed their ambition and revenge, or to gratify the guilty paffions of minions and favourites, at the expence of publick mifery, are fingular objects of Divine refentment, and a ftrange punifhment is prepared for them by the righteous *Avenger*. No man has authority from God for partial advantage, but for the common good. And while God fuffers fuch rulers to hold dominion among men, he utterly abhors the injuftice and wickednefs of their adminiftrations ; he will bring to fwift deftruction thefe haughty oppreffors of the nations, and proportion his plagues to their violence, and to the forrows which they have produced to their fellow men. He will eventually fhew his power, and make his wrath known in their wonderful perdition.

But let none imagine, that God has no gracious purpofes to anfwer by an iniquitous adminiftration of civil government. Infatiable oppreffors, bloody conquerors and imperial butchers, are of ufe in the fcheme of Providence, to correct and amend the revolting tribes of men. While they make the earth to tremble, and turn fruitful fields into a defolate wildernefs, they are the meffengers of divine difpleafure, the rod of God's anger, and the ftaff of his indignation, againft an hypocritical

and

and rebellious people. If a wife and merciful administration will not correct the diffoluteness of an obdurate people, God fcourges them with the flings of fcorpions, with the relentlefs cruelty and ambition of unprincipled tyrants. Such difpenfations are neceffary, both to reclaim the difobedient, and as an example of retributive juftice upon the incorrigible, that others may fhun the rocks on which they fplit.

God's judgments are full of mercy. That greateft temporal calamity which men experience, an unrighteous adminiftration of civil power, has yet a gracious mixture of compaffion, and tends to make perfect the fcheme of Providence.

But a good and equal adminiftration of government, is a bleffing to the community in a different fenfe. The enjoyments and tranquility of fubjects are fecured by the protection of rulers. To advance general happinefs, to fecure property, to increafe true, rational liberty, and to preferve the lives of men, are the original purpofes for which civil laws and magiftrates are ordained by heaven. The Supreme Ruler has given to magiftrates no warrant to purfue unequal or partial meafures; to confult perfonal or family interefts; nor to fofter
the

the wishes and pursuits of cringing favourites.——
The sword of the state is not committed to them
for the exclusive advantage of particular societies
or classes of men. To promote the general good,
to cherish virtue, and to diffuse joyous prosperity
through the whole community, are the ends for
which God has exalted them to power. And they
may pursue the interests of individuals, only in
consistency with the public benefit. The design
of their institution, is to encourage virtue, to protect good men, to frown upon the courses of the
wicked, and to reprefs that fraud and injustice, by
which oppressors consume the faithful of the land,
and devour the widow and him who hath no
helper.

Our Apostle would teach the civil authority,
that the great objects of their care, are to cherish
virtue, and extirpate vice ; to avenge public and
individual wrongs ; to curb the excesses of selfish
avarice and ambition, and to foster that philanthropy and integrity, by which alone, nations can
be built up and established. And they would do
well to remember, that not only the general welfare of the community is a principal object with all
rulers who pursue the end of their appointment,
but that God requires of them, a constant and
watchful

watchful attention to the happiness of the church of Chrift; and for this plain reafon, that magiftrates can in no way fo fubftantially promote the common good, as by honouring the doctrines and followers of Jefus. Whatever infidel wits may dream to the contrary, Jefus Chrift is appointed by the Father to an univerfal kingdom. * *For the Father hath committed all judgment to the Son.* † *And gave him to be head over all things to the Church.* By him Kings reign, and at his pleafure he fets up and cafts down all human rule and authority. And thofe are fhort fighted politicians, who pay no fpecial regard to Chrift. As the Governor of all States, he will be acknowledged Supreme, *fitting in the affemblies of the mighty, and judging among the Gods.* States who have heard of Chrift and his exaltation, and give him no public acknowledgements, are profanely impious againft the Father and the Son, and may well fear the wrath of the Lamb. Let rulers then receive their power, as proceeding from Chrift, and by folemn teftimonies of refpect to him and to his difciples, honour him as their Sovereign: And thus *kifs the Son, left he be angry and they perifh from the way.* They are ordained for the particular benefit of the Church, for the profperity of which, all the wheels of Pro-

C   vidence,

* John, v. 22.   † Eph. 1. 22.

vidence, and all the revolutions of empire, have been in motion from the morning of time. It should lie upon the minds of rulers, especially of those who make a profession, *that they believe the truth of the Christian religion*, to honour Christ by a true profession, and an answerable life, and by their immediate regards in all their administrations, to the prosperity and dignity of Christ's family upon earth. This is God's governing end in their appointment to rule, that his children *may lead peaceable and quiet lives in godliness and honesty*. It is a gross mistake, an affront upon the Lord of all worlds, to affirm, that civil magistrates have nothing to do for the church of Christ. Their paramount Sovereign, has taught them, that they cannot discharge their civil trust, without a diligent attention to his church upon earth. As well may the minister of an earthly Prince alledge, that he has nothing to do for the peace and dignity of his master's family, as civil rulers can alledge, that they have no concern with the church, the family of the King of Zion. The magistrates most assiduous and unwearied labours are due by his appointment to the church of God.

Our attention is called under the next head, to specify,

III.

III. WHAT measures the civil authority muſt purſue, to anſwer the end of their inſtitution.

THE God of Heaven, who ſetteth up Kings, and removeth Kings at his pleaſure, gives to rulers the kingdom, ſtrength, power, and glory, for the benefit of his people. To anſwer this benevolent purpoſe of Heaven, ſhould be the magiſtrates firſt employment. How this purpoſe may be moſt effectually anſwered is our preſent enquiry. And here I ſhall be indulged in ſeveral particulars. And

1ſt, To be the miniſter of God for good, the ruler muſt enterrain an ardent love for his people.

LOVE is the main ſpring of every interchange of kind offices amongſt men. In no caſe has this Divine principle a more efficacious operation, than when the ruler's heart is inſpired with a paternal affection towards his ſubjects. To be the father of his people, is the magiſtrate's dignity: This conſtitutes his neareſt conformity to our univerſal Parent: This will animate him to proſecute the common happineſs, under all temptations, and in ſeaſons of the moſt preſſing trials and difficulties: Without this, he will faint under the perverſeneſs and ingratitude of his people, when they oppoſe his labours for their good, and ill requite his faithful and painful ſervices for national eſta-
blishment

blifhment and profperity. Love animated the patience and perfeverance of Mofes, to plead for Ifraël
in their numerous rebellions, and finally to pledge
his own profperity, for their falvation, when he
prayed that God would fpare them, altho' to vindicate his juftice, he fhould blot him out of his book;
that is, cut him off from a name and inheritance
among the tribes of the Lord, in the land of promife.

THIS noble affection filled David with all the
agonies of diftrefs, and the importunity of prayer,
that God would fpare the fheep of his flock, from
the fword of the deftroying Angel, which was
drawn over Jerufalem. This fortified Nehemiah,
to a life of felf-denial, conflict and danger, while
he built the city of his father's fepulchres. And
this will give energy to the endeavours of all magiftrates for the profperity of their brethren, and
make them to efteem diligence, watchfulnefs, perfonal expence, felf-denial, continual humiliation
and fupplication before God, but reafonable and
pleafant fervices for the public benefit. That
he may purfue their profperity, the ruler muft
cultivate a tender and benevolent affection for his
people.   Again,

  2dly, To be God's minifter for good, the ruler
muft learn the characters and intereft of his people.

                                    IGNORANT

IGNORANT and uninformed Statesmen, however honest in their intentions, can do very little for the happiness of the community. Their limited views create local prejudices, and subject them to the artifices of interested politicians. While a part of the community make undue advantages of their ignorant mismanagement, the body languishes and withers away for want of counsel, energy and uniformity in the civil administration. It concerns rulers, therefore, to be well acquainted with the tempers, capacities, views and interests of the citizens, in all parts of their government, that they may adapt their administration to the advantage of the whole, without material injury to individuals. Rulers unacquainted with the interests of the several professions, and the reputation and capacities of the principal characters, will make grievous mistakes in government, by confining their labours to a narrow circle, and by losing the services of the most suitable men in the community. What is more preposterous, than for rulers to exert their influence and authority, for the partial interest of the territory in their vicinity, to make the interest of one class or profession yield to the avarice and ambition of another ; to be a stickler for this or that faction in the State ? A ruler should have an enlarged heart, a noble, well-inftructed mind ; able to comprehend the characters and interefts of his brethren, and dif-pofed, with a generous impartiality and diffufive benevolence, to fpeak peace to all his feed. And for this end he muft ftudy the difpofitions, the employ-ments, the weakneffes and abilities, and the fub-ftantial interefts of all his fubjects. This know-ledge is effentially requifite to be an ufeful and reputable magiftrate.　　Again,

3dly, To be a minifter for good to the people, the ruler muft be inftructed in the political max-ims and laws of the State, in which he governs.

The fafety of a people, efpecially of a free peo-ple, depends upon a facred adherence to the origi-nal principles of their government.　When thofe principles are difregarded, every bleffing is infe-cure, and the adminiftration degenerates into an arbitrary defpotifm. Therefore rulers fhould un-derftand the fyftem of laws, and thofe forms of adminiftration, to which the people are accuftomed, and conform themfelves to thofe original princi-ples ; then they will have a line of conduct in their office, and the people will know what to ex-pect from them.　As a general knowledge of civil policy is neceffary to make an *accomplifhed* ruler, fo a thorough acquaintance with their own ftate po-licy,

licy, is neceſſary to make a *tolerable* one. When ignorance is in place, the people will mourn, and folly and wickedneſs be exalted on every ſide. It was an eſſential qualification for government in Solomon, * That God had given him *wiſdom and largeneſs of heart, very much, even as the ſand upon the ſea-ſhore.* † *Wo to thee, O land, when thy King is a child.* The curſe of ignorant uninformed rulers, is taught us by the prophet Iſaiah, ‡ *And I will give children to be their Princes, and babes ſhall rule over them : As for my people, children are their oppreſſors, and woman rule over them : O my people, they which lead thee, cauſe thee to err.* And faith Solomon, § *The Prince that wanteth underſtanding, is alſo a great oppreſſor.* But by wiſdom and underſtanding the throne is eſtabliſhed, and the expectations of the people are richly gratified. No man therefore, ſhould undertake to rule amongſt men, until he is fully inſtructed into the civil conſtitution and laws of the community, where he is to govern. Again,

4thly. To promote the public good, rulers muſt be controuled in all their meaſures, by truth and integrity.

For wiſdom without integrity, will ſoon degenerate into cunning and artifice, by which the intereſts of the community will fall a prey to thoſe

who

---

* 1 Kings, iv. 29.   † Ecclef. x. 16.
‡ Iſaiah, iii, 4, 12.   § Prov. xxviii, 16.

who should be their friendly protectors. A magistrate without truth and sincerity, is the snare and perdition of his subjects. All power should be founded in truth, both in the attainment and exercise of it. * *The lip of truth shall be established for-ever : but a lying tongue is but for a moment.* † *Excellent speech becometh not a fool, much less do lying lips a prince.* An administration founded in truth and righteousness, will bear the test of scrutiny : and measures dictated by honesty, shall come forth approved and prosperous in the end : while the duplicity of deceitful politicians shall perish, and involve both rulers and subjects in the snares of perplexity and ruin. All men, especially all leading men, carry their measures with the most success and reputation, when they prosecute them with simple uniformity and honest sincerity. It should therefore be the first object with him who rules over men, to be just, to be true in his administrations : not having a mysterious system of delusion to deceive others into his fraudulent intentions.

To gain the confidence of their subjects, rulers must be men upon whom they may safely depend. And without this confidence, subjects can derive very little advantage from government. Men in place,

* Prov. xiii. 19.   † Prov. xvii. 7.

place, therefore, muſt make declarations and promiſes ſtrictly juſt and clearly intelligible, and by
adhering to them, the ſubject muſt know what to
expect from authority. Rulers, to be uſeful, muſt
deal fairly and honeſtly with the people ; diſtribute
equal juſtice ; protect them from wrongs, and
puniſh injuries with integrity and deciſion : not
leave honeſt men the prey of fraud.

It is a ſad time, when rulers are ſo inattentive to
juſtice and veracity, that truth falleth in the ſtreets,
and he who departeth from iniquity, maketh him-
ſelf a prey. Good rulers make fair promiſes and
keep them, and are exemplary in fulfiling contracts. The magiſtrate who defrauds his ſubjects,
will have a poor face to puniſh individuals who
defraud one another. Do rulers wiſh to be public bleſſings? then let them keep good the public
faith, ſuſtain the credit of the ſtate, and pay
punctually the public contracts. This will give
energy to government, eſtabliſh the influence and
credit of authority, and teach the people that up-
rightneſs and veracity, by which alone the various
members of ſociety can be cloſely cemented. A
diſſembler and a cheat among individuals, is a baſe
character ; and a fraudulent adminiſtration of government, is a character as much more deteſtible,
as the number and authority of the rulers exceed

D one

one individual. Some have acted as though a fraud or falsehood might be lost in the number of partners, or be sanctified by great and powerful names : But he who sitteth in the Heavens, will manifest their error, and prove, ** *that lying lips are an abomination to the Lord, that they are but for a moment,* that the feet of unrighteous rulers stand in slippery places; and when the good man seeth their end, he shall suddenly curse their habitation. Does the ruler wish to be useful and reputable ? Let him be a true and honest man. Would he involve himself and the community in infamy and perplexity? Let him be unequal in his administrations ; let his performances contradict his promises ; by false weights and false measures of justice and equity, let him frame iniquity by law, and teach the Lord's people to transgress. Again,

5thly, To rule well, the magistrate must cultivate habits of industry and frugality.

RULERS have so much to do, that they have no time to lose. An indolent ruler, like the useless and unwieldly drone, devours the honey which others have gathered. He consumes the people's tribute without earning it. The support which subjects

* Prov. xii. 22.

subjects should liberally furnish for the maintenance of government, rulers should merit by their diligent services. And while they carefully avoid avarice in witholding expences for the public good, it concerns them to use the revenues of the State, with œconomy, that no part of the public treasure be applied, to useless and trifling purposes. Covetousness and prodigality are both mischievous vices in rulers, and they should avoid each extreme, if they would be blessings to the people.

INDOLENT rulers will be otherways vicious. Idleness will cloud their minds and extinguish the nobler sensations of the soul, and the most noxious weeds will spring up in their place. By their example, habits of idleness, intemperance, dissipation, gaming and profaneness, like some infectious contagion, will spread through all ranks of people. An enervated, poor and contemptible people will be the consequence of an indolent and dissipated administration of government. Such wicked rulers will rule over a poor, worthless people ; the community will sink into effeminacy, dependance and wretchedness. It becomes the magistrate then to be a man of business, not a man of pleasure ; to be attentive to his office, and painful in his exertions for the common good. Thus shall his ex-

ample

ample recommend hardiness, patience, frugality and self-denial to his subjects; and through the prevalence of these virtues, they shall be able to meet the enemy in the gate, and rise with lustre among the nations. It was the maxim of a Grecian Prince, worthy to be adopted by the Christian magistrate, *It ill becomes a Statesman, to sleep all night.*

THE virtues of industry, and well-judged frugality, are the support of republican governments, and are therefore peculiarly requisite in their civil authority, who by their example, should teach the people habits of diligence, hardiness and œconomy, not to consume, according to the baneful customs of our republics, in dissipation and luxury, much more than we earn by our labour, and industry. Again,

6thly, To answer the purpose of their institution, civil rulers must protect good citizens, and punish the wicked.

THE scripture character of rulers is, *That they are not a terror to good works, but to the evil.* Power is grossly abused and perverted, when wicked citizens are fostered and protected by authority. God has ordained rulers to avenge the wrongs of injustice and oppression, and the violences of sedition and rebellion. It is only when bad men are in authority,

thority, that vile men are exalted and screened from justice. No favour or friendship, no relation or connection with men in power, should cover the wicked from punishment. Rulers are to execute the laws : And the laws are made for the lawless and disobedient. All delays of justice, the exemption from chastisement, which corrupt citizens receive in breaking the peace and violating the ordinances of justice, is a sore malady in the State, and proves that the head is sick and the heart faint. Good magistrates, by their influence, suppress immorality, and every transgression of relative justice. God commands it; and faithful subjects have a claim upon their rulers, to be protected from fraud and oppression, to have the laws executed, their persons, their liberty and property protected, from the depredations of designing and unprincipled men. And the magistrate who does not endeavour to punish and reclaim, or utterly to purge from the State wicked and disobedient subjects, forgets the main design of his exaltation. And when good men are left to the fear and danger of losing their privileges and possessions, they are sadly neglected ; and the God of Heaven, will avenge their quarrel against such slothful and unrighteous magistrates. To let the wicked

go

go unpunished, and the righteous live without protection, is both a contemptible weakness and a scandalous wickedness in authority. * *For it should be an abomination to Kings to do wickedness, and the throne is established by righteousness.* † *Righteousness exalteth a nation, but sin is the reproach of any people.* ‡ *He that justifieth the wicked, and he that condemneth the just, even they both are abomination to the Lord.* For this end rulers wait upon their work to make a clear distinction between the just and the unjust; and it is an illustrious display of benevolence, to over-whelm incorrigible offenders by the arm of power, and raise to safety and honour the faithful of the land. It is a precept grounded upon moral reasons, and consequently of perpetual obligation,—§ *The man that will do presumptuously and will not hearken unto the Priest, which standeth there to minister before the Lord thy God, or unto the judge, even that man shall die; and thou shall put away the evil from Israel.* The State must employ punishments adequate to the suppression of vice, and rewards commensurate to the encouragement of virtue and fidelity: And the ruler who permits the rod of the wicked to rest upon the lot of the righteous, is disobedient to God, and an enemy to his people. Again, 7thly.

* Prov. xvi. 12. † Prov. xiv. 34.
‡ Prov. xvii. 15. § Deut. xvii. 12.

7thly, RULERS, to be minifters of God for good, muft be men of religion.

ALL chriftian graces are of immediate ufe in the adminiftration of government. And as rulers receive their ordination from God, he expects that as fervants they honour him, and obey his Son Jefus Chrift, as their liege Lord. Since religion, furnifhes men with thofe excelling gifts and good difpofitions, which qualify them to govern, fo they can never cultivate faith and piety with too careful an affiduity. Their fuccefs in office, and their ufefulnefs among their fubjects, depend primarily upon the Divine prefence and bleffing. Therefore they fhould be men of exemplary faith in their King and Saviour, and not lean unto their own underftanding. That illuftrious magiftrate Nehemiah, thought it a moft effential qualification in his brother Hananiah, to take charge over Jerufalem. * *Becaufe he was a faithful man and feared God above many.* Magiftrates fhould be men of prayer, that God may dwell with them and direct their counfels. They fhould be accuftomed to appear before God in the pofture of fuppliants, that he would enlighten their ignorance, and profper their exertions. None have more need of wifdom, than they ; and to whom fhould they apply

ply

* Neh. vii. 2.

ply but to him *who giveth to all men liberally, and up-braideth not.* Would they be honoured by the obedience of their subjects ? Let them obtain this honour by obeying God, by lives of temperance, sobriety and a becoming gravity. Like their blessed Master; let them be meek, humble and gentle towards all men ; like him, love righteousness and hate iniquity, be constant, watchful and fervant in duty, bearing the sorrows, and relieving the distresses of their fellow men ; like him *go about doing good.* It is incumbent upon them, to honor Christ in his institutions, setting a pattern before their brethren of family religion, resolving with the pious and valiant Joshua, That as for us and our houses, we will serve the Lord ; attending uniformly upon the ordinances of public worship, hallowing God's Sabbaths, and reverencing his sanctuary, attentively waiting upon the dispensation of the gospel. From rulers we may well expect submission to all God's commandments, and that they cherish the appointed means of diffusing christian knowledge, and by honouring Christ's ministers and followers, become *nursing fathers to the Church.* Some have thought that religion is no important part of a ruler's character : It is true, that rulers without religion are to be obeyed. But when it is considered

dered

dered that they are made rulers ultimately for the good and prosperity of the Church, we must censure those for their ignorance or irreligion, who adopt a maxim so pernicious to civil society, and embarraffing to the interefts of virtue and morality. Without religion, rulers have no God, unto whom they may repair and expect his blefling upon their adminiftration. God is not with them, and when his prefence is withdrawn, darknefs and perplexity will fill their paths with fnares and adverfity. Immoral and ungodly rulers may affect courtefy, affability and patriotifm to gain popularity ; but they have no moral principle upon which the public may depend, and too often have they proved the fcourge of the community, and the rod of God's indignation againft a profane or hypocritical people. Therefore we lay it down as a qualification of great moment to the State, that magiftrates be men of piety, who have a governing regard to the glory of God, and a warm affection for the gofpel of Chrift. Such are the fentiments avowed in our form of government, which requires the great officers of government, before they enter upon their truft, to declare their belief of the Chriftian religion, as the religion taught from Heaven, for the happinefs and falvation of loft men. Again,

E   8thly,

8thly, To influence them to a useful discharge of their trust, it is important, that rulers keep in mind their mortality and their future account before the bar of God.

* *I have said, ye are Gods : and all of you are children of the Most High. But ye shall die like men.* Like their brethren of the dust they shall go to the grave, *the house appointed for all the living.* To death succeeds their solemn account at the tribunal of the son of man, *who will judge the secrets of men according to our gospel.* The wise, the great and the mighty of the earth, will stand before the impartial judgement-seat, upon a level with the despised and indigent of their subjects. At that solemn hour when the opinions of men shall be lighter than the dust of the balance, and the flattering tongue shall be put to perpetual silence, when the judgment shall be the Lord's and shall be administered without respect of persons, the enquiry will be, not whether we have been great in the earth, enjoyed the applauses of our fellow worms, and exercised dominion among the sons of the dust : but whether we have filled our station, kept in view our last account, and prepared matters for our acquittal at the solemn trial. Rulers should remember that their reward will be in

exact

* Psalm. lxxxii. 6 7.

exact proportion to their benevolence and fidelity, not according to their power and authority ; and that their punishment will not be alleviated by any instances of present impunity from the impotence of human justice : but according to their sloth and luxury, their wantonness and ambition, their oppression and avarice, such will be their retribution from the sentence of the Lord of Sabaoth, who hears the groans of injured and neglected subjects, and has prepared a strange punishment for the haughty oppressors of the earth.

WERE this day of retribution, which will soon overtake us all, duely realized by magistrates, how could they fail to discharge with assiduity and care their sacred trust, and to be in earnest to become ministers of God for good, to the people ? Having stated the methods, by which rulers may answer the benevolent purposes of Heaven in their appointment, it concerns us under the last general head,

IV. To point out the obligations of subjects to the civil authority.

IT is the prerogative of a free people to appoint men from among their brethren to rule over them. It is their duty and only security to use this prerogative with discretion and fidelity, * *not using their liberty*

* 1 Pet. ii. 16.

liberty as a cloak of maliciousness, but as the servants of God. They are required to look out from among them, chosen and faithful men, who know the times, men of unshaken integrity and fortitude, of industry and temperance, who love their nation, and are examples of gentleness and philanthropy, *who fear God and hate covetousness.* When they have appointed their rulers, both obligation and interest require them to be in subjection to them, as the ordinance of God; and under them to lead peaceable and quiet lives, in all godliness and honesty. They should strengthen the hands of their rulers in the work of government, treat with liberality their administrations, and studiously avoid a mean spirit of jealousy and suspicion, that bane of society and destruction of public blessings. A haughty, unyielding and murmuring disposition, is the infamy of subjects, and will prove their eventual ruin from the justice of God, who wills that his ordinances be respected by men. They *who despise government, are pre-sumptuous, self-willed, and are not afraid to speak evil of dignities, and speak evil of things which they know not,* have little sense of their duty to magistrates, are disturbers of the public peace, and *shall utterly perish in their own corruption.* * The word of inspiration testifies to us the will of Christ, respecting the obligations of subjects to civil authority. It is

* II. Pet. ii. 10, 12.

is a leading duty, That subjects pray for their rulers, and offer up in public and private, acknowledgements for the blessings of government, and supplications for Divine favour upon the civil administration. Saith the Apostle, *I exhort therefore, that first of all, supplications, prayers, intercessions and giving thanks, be made for all men. For Kings and for all that are in authority ; that we may live a peaceable and quiet life, in all godliness and honesty. For this is good and acceptable in the sight of God our Saviour.* It is a Divine injunction, †*Submit yourselves to every ordinance of man for the Lord's sake ; whether it be unto the King as supreme, or unto Governours as unto them that are sent by him for the punishment of evil doers, and for the praise of them that do well. For it is the will of God, that with well doing, ye put to silence the ignorance of foolish men. Fear God, honour the King.* If kingly government deserves such conscientious obedience, how much more does a free government deserve it ? It is required of Christian ministers to inculcate this duty upon their hearers. ‡ " *Put them in mind to be subject to principalities and powers, to obey magistrates, to be ready to every good work.* All who hope in his mercy, and would be saved by the righteousness of Christ, must imitate that example of submission to civil authority, which in his life he hath set

before

* 1 Tim. ii. 1, 2, 3.   † 1 Pet. ii. 13.   ‡ Titus, iii. 1.

before them ; not by ambition and turbulent
paffions, difturb the quiet of fociety ; not by tumults and fedition augment the miferies of this
miferable world. Men who have not a temper
of fubordination, are not charitable, humble and
quiet in their demeanor, are poorly qualified for
heaven. Men who refift lawful authority, and
are engaged in tumults and confufion, may be fit
for the realms of anarchy, darknefs and defpotifm ;
but without repentance they fhall never behold
the feats of the bleffed, where every man is con-
tent with his ftation. Do we wifh for prefent
fecurity and enjoyment, for national ftrength and
dignity ? Do we wifh to behold the feats of the
bleffed ? Then we muft obey magiftrates.

I HAVE finifhed my doctrinal obfervations ; may
I be indulged in fome practical reflections, and
fundry curfory obfervations upon the prefent
fituation of this Commonwealth, and the methods
which God requires to be purfued for reftoring
and lengthening out our tranquility, and then
conclude with addreffes fuited to this important
occafion. As I have endeavoured in the whole,
fo in this branch of difcourfe I would wifh to fpeak
with the unfettered freedom of a Servant of that
Prince, *whofe Kingdom is not of this world.*

THIS

THIS country was planted by men of fingular piety, of whom the old world was not worthy. God found them a refuge from the oppreffion of civil and fpiritual tyranny. Having planted, he protected them from the moft preffing dangers. Often hath he delivered them by figns and wonders, and by an out-ftretched arm. In fome feeble mea-fure our Forefathers lived worthy of the Divine care over them, and by grateful obedience ac-knowledged the falvations wrought for them. But their children forgat his benefits, and by ir-religion and fenfuality; by diffipation and luxury, by worldlinefs and pride, they provoked the Holy One of Ifrael, to threaten them with the lofs of thofe privileges and bleffings; which he had fo richly beftowed, and they had fo unthankfully abufed.

MANY have celebrated the virtues, and confi-dently predicted the rifing glories of the American States. But while we continue our provocations, we may do well to enquire, Whether thefe flat-tering panegyrifts *do not fpeak to us fmooth things, and prophefy deceits ?* Would not the fublime prophet Ifaiah addrefs us in another ftile ? * " *Hear O heavens, and give ear O earth ! for the Lord hath fpoken. I have nourifhed and brought up children, and they have rebelled againft me. Ah finful nation, a people laden*
with

Ifaiah i. 2, 4.

with iniquity, a feed of evil doers, children that are corrupters, they have forfaken the Lord, they have provoked the Holy One of Ifrael unto anger, they have gone away backward. Becaufe the Lord was wroth with his heritage, he did of late raife up adverfaries unto them of their brethren. The Britifh parliament, in fupport of a groundlefs claim, levied an unnatural war againft us, and affumed without warrant to be the Higher Powers in our governments.

By the will of God, and the direction of his ordinance, our civil authority, to whom our firft allegiance was due, we were called to contend for our poffeffions, our liberties and our lives, even unto blood. Long and diftreffing was the conflict. In the confufions of war, and efpecially in the perplexities of fuch a war, in which the minds of the people were divided as to their duties of allegiance, order and government were effentially injured amongft us, and that fpirit of fubordination and loyalty, which was before habitual, was nearly loft, and for a feafon we were threatened with all the miferies of that people, who have no magiftrate to put them in fear. But in the feafon of our declenfions, He who remembereth mercy for his people, interpofed for our help, and in due time ordained peace for us. But in nothing

was

was his grace more remarkable, than in leading us out of a diftempered ftate of partial anarchy into a ftate of order and government. He gave us laws and teftimonies right and good, a civil conftitution perhaps the moft perfect in the world, which is the fecurity of good citizens, the admiration of the wife, and the envy of tyrants : To which if if we ftrictly adhere, we cannot in a political fenfe, fail of being a happy people.

Since this mercy of our God upon us, in faving us from the evils of war, and plucking us from the confufions of anarchy, we have walked unworthy of his great goodnefs. We fang his praifes, but foon forgot his benefits. We have continued to indulge thofe follies and excefles, for which he had already chaftized us. While deeply involved in debt, our diftempered paffion for the fashions of luxurious and affluent nations, plunged us into our former prodigality and unprofitable expences. Inftead of applying ourfelves to difcharge the claims of public and private creditors, and thus to vindicate our honour and independence, we employed the riches of our foil in purchafing the trappings of an exotic drefs, and in indulging our vitiated appetites in the expenfive productions of diftant regions, and thus are we become the fervants of foreigners, and ftrangers

F

rule

rule over us. Poor and dependent, our minds are enervated to the pursuits of national freedom and dignity. And yet restless under the unavoidable pressure of our follies, we are little inclined to satisfy our creditors, and pay the price of our beloved dissipation. Like the prodigal, exhausted and worn down by riot, we complain of our pains and embarrassments, and idly resolve into a grievance, that poverty, from which no created power but our own can save us. Jaded by our vices, indigent through profuse living, rendered untractable by long exemption from the restraints of human and Divine laws, and proud in a licentious liberty, that fore-runner of despotism, we have become restless under necessary burdens, and with a mistaken resentment, have complained of public requisitions as the source of our sorrows and perplexities. Lavish expences have made us poor, and a temper not duly subordinate, has turned our complaints from our own follies, against our Fathers, our best friends and benefactors. How many of us have laboured to free ourselves from the necessary burdens of public and private debts, that we might obtain a wider scope for the indulgence of appetites, which it were much better to mortify?

WILL the enquiry be thought immodest, when I ask, whether our wealthy and leading characters,
have

have not been first in this transgression ? Of the legislators of our republican government, we might have expected effectual laws to discourage excesses, by which the citizens are so certainly degraded to a state of servility and dependence. They knew better than their constituents, the evil of such excesses. Might they not in due season, have encouraged industry, temperance and frugality, among the people ; laid restrictions upon foreign luxuries, and made it as necessary as it was useful, for the people to produce the accommodations of life by their own labour, and upon their own soil. And especially might not the examples of men in power, and families of fashion and affluence, in preferring the productions of our own country, to commodities received from abroad, have produced the most salutary effects among all classes of our citizens ? Such examples would have been more influential and authoritative, than a whole code of commercial regulations. This is one of our wounds ; I mention it freely, since I hope in a good Providence, that our rulers, our public teachers and the multitude of our brethren, will think it important to apply themselves to a radical cure of the evil. For nothing kills the noble spirit of freedom, like a state of dependence, which

will

will ever attend the folly of spending more than we earn. Let our rulers not merely in word, but in deed, by a laudable example, be first in this matter, and teach republicans to be honeft, induftrious and frugal in their modes of living. Then fhall fubftantial wealth and independence be the joyous portion, of all claffes of our happy citizens.

THAT we have been tranfgreffors in many moral and Chriftian duties, the God of judgement hath teftified, in the calamities brought upon us. To punifh and to reclaim us, he hath fent among us the rod of his vifitation. * *Shall there be evil in the city, and the Lord hath not done it?*

THE laft year, a year equally diftinguifhed for the gifts of Providence, and for our unthankfulnefs and difobedience to human and Divine authority, has been fruitful in new and perplexing evils. God has fuffered a fpirit of infurrection and refiftance of lawful authority to rife up in this Commonwealth. As a correction from him, it is a righteous teftimony of his holy difpleafure ; as proceeding from man, perhaps an oppofition to government, and a war againft the community, has been feldom more wanton and unprovoked.

The

* Amos, iii. 6.

The objects fought after, in these tumults, have been of the most faulty kind. One avowed end was to compel the Legiflature, into an emiffion of a paper currency, to be a tender in payment of all public and private contracts. A meafure wholly prepofterous, when the public ought to be difcharging their old obligations, and not contracting a new debt by borrowing money by an emiffion of paper ; a meafure totally unjuft, and as truly impolitic as to adminifter opiates to cure a lethargy. The faultinefs of fuch violent attempts arofe alfo from the utter impoffibility in the prefent ftate of our affairs, that the Legiflature could make a promife upon their paper and keep it ; that is, they could never honeftly redeem the money, by faving it from a rapid depreciation, and making punctual payment. Such a meafure then, would have been a grofs violation of commutative juftice, the unwavering obfervance of which, is enjoined upon all bodies of men under all poffible circumftances. To endeavour by hoftility to compel the Legiflature into a meafure, which they wifely thought impolitic, and knew to be palpably unjuft, was an high handed offence, and clearly proves, that multitudes were under the clouds of God's anger, and were fadly forfaken of reftraining grace. BUT

But the defign was filled with other mifchiefs. It was to wreft from the Legiflature the power of governing; from the tribunals of law the power of decreeing juftice; and from the Executive, the effential prerogative of carrying into effect the laws of the Commonwealth. Thus were our foundations to have been deftroyed. The declared intentions of the male-contents, and what they attempted by levying an impious war upon their country, was to arreft the arm of government, and feize the adminiftration of a defpotic rule into their own hands; to fap the foundations of our glorious conftitution, to change its effential forms, and thus to break down the barriers of our rights, and overwhelm this great republic in dreary confufion and irretrievable ruin. Whoever has been acquainted with their complaints and their claims, and has been the witnefs of their proceedings, will confider this, as a charitable reprefentation of their views and purfuits.

Blessed be the Lord God of our falvation, that in the midft of our unworthinefs and provocations, he has interpofed and faved us from the fword of the oppreffor, and the violence of wicked men. Ardent thankfgivings are this day due to
the

the Father of mercies, That in the feason of alarming dangers, he raifed up an adminiftration of government, who, in the faithful page of hiftory, will be celebrated for their wifdom, their moderation and integrity.

AFTER many outrageous and treafonable exceffes had prevailed, in feveral parts of the State, and the lives and eftates of their guilty authors were forfeited to their country, our Chief Magiftrate, at the requeft of the Legiflature, offered a free and full pardon to all the promoters and abettors of thofe feditious tumults. Through an infatuated obduracy, that pardon was fcornfully rejected, even under the cleareft light and evidence exhibited to them, that their complaints were groundlefs, and that the government had been adminiftered with great integrity. Former violences were renewed, the criminal demands of the infurgents increafed, and the exiftence of the Commonwealth, was put to the hazard. When unmixed mercy could not reclaim but raifed to higher exceffes the refiftance of the offenders, authority affumed a more firm and decifive tone, and raifed a military force to repel their violence. Yet great was the forbearance and compaffion of government in all their exertions to fupprefs the rebellion. Forgivenefs was still extended

tended to the body of the rebels, the leaders only were left to the justice of the law, and even with the leaders much lenity was used by proffering terms of pardon to many of them. The steps of our civil administration were the marks of their justice and humanity. The wisdom and decision of the Council, demand our admiration and gratitude : the measures of our Chief Magistrate all denoted the firmness of his spirit, his regard for our laws, his inflexible adherence to the principles of the constitution, and his unshaken determination to protect his country, and repress the violence of wicked men. His conduct was equally distinguished for benignity and moderation, that aversion from bloodshed and that ardent wish to recover and preserve offenders, which is a shining part of the character of a good man and a christian magistrate. He hath shewed himself *the* FATHER *and* FRIEND *of his country. The minister of God for good to his people.*

THAT worthy personage who acted under his immediate orders in suppressing the public commotions, has added fresh laurels to his former honors, and evinced how much he deserves the appellation of the CHRISTIAN HERO. The officers and men employed in this important and unwelcome service, fervice, by their firm, temperate and wife conduct, difcovered that excellent fpirit which ought ever to reign in the bofoms of free citizens. Ye authors and leaders of thefe happy operations, if we forget your fervices, let our right hand forget its cunning. Thou country *thus* faved of the Lord from the horns of the unicorn, if we do not remember thee above our chief joy, let our tongue cleave to the roof of our mouth.

Thrones of judgement are eftablifhed, and the feat of violence is driven from us : and by the uninterrupted execution of our wholefome laws, we may fit quietly under our own vines and under our own fig-trees. And we may gladly hope, that without connivance from men of influence, thefe feeds of fedition will e'er long be totally eradicated from our republic. The methods of Providence in protecting the Commonwealth and fucceeding the meafures of government, merit particular notice and unfeigned gratitude. The finger of God has been confpicuous in directing and profpering our public counfels. Operations dictated by wifdom and moderation, have been fucceeded by remarkable interpofitions of Heaven. The hearts of thofe in rebellion melted like wax, and they

G   could

could perform no part of their enterprize ; and the meafures of adminiftration were crowned with the wifhed for fuccefs.

May the author of all effectual influences imprefs the minds of deluded citizens with a conviction of the criminality of their conduct, and of the evident hand of God, which was lifted up againft them. It is but juftice to obferve, that the meafures of government, have been conformable to the fyftem of God's government over a finful world. Mercy has been freely proffered, and when defpifed, has been followed by a mixture of judgement and mercy. Becaufe the Lord loved his people, he hath inclined the hearts of their rulers into fuch a profperous and falutary adminiftration. To regard thefe foot-fteps of Providence, and purfue a fimilar fyftem of adminiftration, can fcarcely fail to recover us from our confufions, and eftablifh our public tranquility. But inattention to the finger of God, and an abufe of his healing mercies, the continuance of our rebellions and refiftance of his civil ordinance, will provoke him to empty us from veffel to veffel, *and for the iniquities of our land, many will be the rulers thereof : unftable as water we fhall not excel.* But if confcious of paft ingratitude and abufe of bleffings, we will turn unto him by

repentance

repentance and works of righteoufnefs, will fpeak the truth one to another and love as brethren ; if our rulers will go before us in the duties of prayer, faith and obedience, fubmiffion to Chrift, and refpect to his doctrines and inftitutions ; if they will love the people and confult their intereft by integrity and goodnefs, ftudy rather to do them good than to gratify their idle humours ; if they will meafure their adminiftrations by the line of truth and honefty, although thoufands frown ; if they will be temperate and induftrious in their work, will punifh the wicked and protect obedient fubjects, and thus fet the Lord alway before their face, then fhall their reputation flourifh and their authority prove an unfpeakable bleffing to the people : * *God fhall fill Zion with judgement and righteoufnefs, and wifdom and knowledge fhall be the ftability of our times and ftrength of falvation : And the fear of the Lord fhall be our treafure ; and he fhall lift us high among the nations.*

The time calls me to a conclufion, in fuitable addreffes.

Our firft attention is due to our worthy Chief Magiftrate, called by God and his country to the chair of government.

May

---

* Ifaiah xxxiii. 5, 6.

May it please your Excellency,

THAT happy tranquillity which we enjoyed under your former adminiſtration, cannot fail to excite our congratulations, that God has ſo far reſtored your health, that you are able to accept the Chief Magiſtracy in this Commonwealth. Appointed by God to bear rule over your brethren, you will be pleaſed to accept our beſt wiſhes that your health may be adequate to the weighty burthens of your high and ſacred office. Our prayer to the Almighty is, that he would be the health of your countenance and your God ; that he would ſtrengthen you to eminent uſefulneſs among his people. May divine preſervation and illumination accompany your adminiſtrations, that you may continue to act worthily for Chriſt our King, and be accepted of the multitude of your brethren. May that diffuſive love which you ſo early manifeſted for your country, by placing yourſelf in the firſt rank of dangers, to repel foreign uſurpation, and vindicate the privileges and laws of your country, ſtill animate you, to purſue the happineſs of the community, by ſupporting the dignity of civil authority, the prerogatives and independence of the Supreme Executive, and the other branches of adminiſtration ; by making law terrible to all invaders and uſurpers of the powers

of

of government, and by drawing a line of diftinc‑
tion between faithful fubjects, and thofe who may
be fo loft to virtue, as to difturb the public peace,
and affail the property, the liberties and the lives
of their fellow‑citizens.

WITH pleafing anticipation, we behold your
Excellency God's minifter for good, bearing the
fword of the State, not as a terror to good works,
but to the evil. Our eye with delight marks your
path, while you lead us your children into the
duties of relative and Chriftian life, and by your
example teach us, that felf‑denial, frugality and
induftry, fo effential to the happinefs of a free
people. From your Excellency, will our Legiflature
expect advice in thofe meafures, which may main‑
tain inviolate the principles of our civil conftitution
againft every fpecies of encroachment ; how the
public good is to be purfued, honefty and integrity,
diligence and application encouraged, and diffi‑
pation driven from the State ; how the laws of
juftice may be effectually vindicated, and the feat
of fraud and oppreffion, be removed far from us.
Our expectations are from your Excellency, That
liberty fhall be maintained by law, and all fubjects
be fecure in their poffeffions ; that public faith,
and national credit and dignity, be follicitoufly
preferved.

MAY

MAY the inftitutions of literature flourifh under your friendly patronage ; efpecially may that illuftrious univerfity to which the public is fo much indebted for laying the foundation of fcience in your Excellency, and qualifying you for fuch extenfive fervices in this, and through the United States, be the object of your peculiar care, and by your powerful influence be protected in all its important rights and immunities.

WE hope in the goodnefs of the univerfal Parent, that by affording you his prefence and grace, he will fhew, that becaufe he loved his people, he hath therefore appointed you to rule over them. From your Excellency, the interefts of piety and the Chriftian religion, juftly expect continual aid and friendly countenance. May the Angel of the Divine prefence, enlighten and beautify the paths of your adminiftration. In your days, religion, truth and peace dwell on the earth, and after you have ferved your generation by the will of God, may you receive the rewards of your fidelity, from the approbation of your Judge. May you here enjoy a portion, better than many fons, and late be welcomed to the prefence of your Divine Saviour and Judge, and from him obtain that Crown of glory which fadeth not away.

OUR

Our respects are now due to the Gentlemen who compose the Honourable the Senate, and the Honourable the House of Representatives.

Fathers of our country, and Elders of our tribes,

YOU are this day constituted by Jesus Christ, the ordinance of God, for the good of his church, and the welfare of this Commonwealth. The oath of God is upon you, to maintain the laws of the State, and the sacred principles of our excellent constitution : A constitution which wisdom will approve, as the national bulwark of our independence and sovereignty, the effectual protection of good citizens, the security of freedom, property and life. and our defence against the rude encroachments of anarchy and despotism. You have this day declared your belief of the Christian religion. Integrity in this profession will lead you to prize our constitution the more, since it is so friendly to morality, and the Christian faith. You have bound yourselves in the discharge of your office, to promote the common good upon gospel principles ; by cultivating in your temper, and practice, those benevolent graces of Christianity, which will enable you to rule with reputation to yourselves, and advantage to the people. You have pledged yourselves to honor Christ's institutions, to protect his servants, to discountenance all contempt of the doctrines

and

and maxims of his holy faith. Thus from the manner of your inauguration, we may expect, that you be nurfing Fathers to the Church. It becomes a minifter of that Church, (and will therefore be acceptable to you) to ftir up your pure minds to ufe the gift that is in you, for the good of the people. You are the Minifters of God, and as fuch, accountable at the tribunal of the Son of Man, in the great day of dread decifion. Let me exhort you as candidates for eternity, to keep in mind that folemn day, and as faithful fervants, to be habitually prepared for it. And that through Divine grace, you may give up a good account at laft, be entreated to regard the eye of God, which is upon you, and look to him to pardon your unworthinefs, to counfel you by his unerring wifdom, and to quicken you by his truth : That he would not take his Holy Spirit from you, but by his effectual influences, guide you into the paths of uprightnefs. The fcriptures will teach you your liablenefs to err; and your defire to be ufeful, will excite your applications for that anointing of the Holy One, by which you will not err fatally. As Rulers, it concerns you to be men of prayer, to maintain an intercourfe with Heaven, and an humble dependance upon Divine teaching and guidance. Do you wifh to be honoured of God in your office? You muft honour him by fubmit-
ing

ing your adminiftrations to his government, by
a refpect to his name, his inftitutions and thofe
eternal laws of righteoufnefs, ordained for the
careful obfervance of all his rational fubjects.
With you *the fear of the Lord is the beginning of
wifdom, and to depart from evil is underftanding.*—
To you as their Fathers, will the people look for
patterns of moral and Chriftian duty. You will
therefore go before them in perfonal, in family
and public religion and obedience. Care for the
State will arm your zeal and fortitude againft
vicious and immoral practices, to frown upon
grofs breaches of human and Divine laws. Your
fervices will be approved of God, and ufeful
to the community, whenever you fhall punifh
with decifion and impartiality, the lawlefs
practices of vicious and difobedient fubjects.
Through your example and official exertions fhall
thofe virtues of benevolence, integrity, induftry
and frugality, fo effential to a republican and
Chriftian community, greatly prevail. And your
teftimony fhall fupprefs the infolence of fraud and
injuftice, falfhood and perjury, by which the bonds
of fociety are diffolved. May the oath of God
become terrible, and all human promifes and contracts be held facred. Punctuality in Rulers to
their contracts, is the firft ftep towards a general

honefty

honefty in the State. Their example gives energy to laws againft private fraud and injuftice. You will feel the bond of that law of your Mafter, *to owe no man any thing* ; but according to the ability of the people, to make a punctual and fatisfactory payment of public debts. You will utterly dif-allow all meafures, which may put honeft and feeble citizens into the power of griping and un-principled oppreffors; than fuch meafures, nothing is more repugnant to that Gofpel, by which you are to be judged. Every indirect method to ex-tricate the people from embarraffments, is a new load to fink them in the mire. The Fathers of our tribes will therefore cultivate public and pri-vate faith, and learn us all *not to go beyond, or to defraud our neighbour.*

MAY the good God influence our honourable Legiflature, into a fyftem of adminiftration, which fhall defend our Conftitution, render venerable our laws, protect from violence the feats of Juftice and the Throne of Judgement, and by a due mixture of mercy and juftice, allure offenders to obedience, or by adequate penalties incapaci-tate them from difturbing the public tranquility. You will think nothing too much to encourage a fpirit of loyalty and patriotifm; and to this end you will

encourage

encourage the means of grace and education. To your wifdom does it belong to difcover the political meafures, for promoting the good defigns which have been mentioned, but I may fuggeft, that they fhould be fuch as are approved by the gofpel of Chrift.

Our national concerns, as a confederated Republic, are ferious concerns. Your deliberate counfels will be requifite to invent fome remedy for our national imbecility and reproach. Unlefs effectual and liberal meafures are foon taken, our glory and independence will vanifh into air. Be intreated Fathers, to lay afide limited views and local prejudices, and to encompafs the Union in the exertions of your wifdom and patriotifm.

The better to anfwer the ends of your appointment, you will confider it highly important, in filling up the vacancies in the Legiflature, and in conftituting a Council for His Excellency, to choofe faithful and approved men, who fear God and obey Chrift above many, men of noble minds, fuperiour to intrigue, and unfettered by faction, of independent fentiments, who abhor covetous practices, men whofe circumftances are not embarraffed, and who will not fear to do the thing
which

which is juft, who love the people, and will by perfonal labours and felf-denial, and unwearied diligence, purfue their folid and lafting advantages, and yet difdain by meannefs and artifice, and by facrificing their own judgement, to gain an empty, popular applaufe.

A LEGISLATURE thus conftituted, and what a refpectable number of fuch amiable and worthy characters do I now behold ; fuch a Legiflature, fhall in the iffue enjoy the bleffings of their country, while time ferving politicians, fhall fink in the dirt of their deferved ignominy : Such a Legiflature may hope to have God with them, to profper the work of their hands. From the faithful difcharge of an earthly truft, they fhall in their time and order, be received to the plaudit of their final Judge. Such is the reward which we pray that every member of our public adminiftration, in the Executive, Legiflative and Judicial department, may now deferve, and in future obtain from the mouth of him, who fiteth upon the Throne.

MAY we all repent, and do our firft works, that God may be in the midft of us. That he may fit in the affembly of our Rulers, is the devout fupplication of all, who hope in his mercy, and wifh well to this Commonwealth.

BLESSED

BLESSED art thou O Land, when thy King is the Son of nobles, and thy Princes eat in due feafon. *Happy is* that people, that is in fuch a cafe ; yea happy is that people, whofe God is the Lord.

THUS with fincerity, and as well as I was able, have I fpoken unto you the Lord's meffage. May the effectual co-operations of the Bleffed Spirit, render the truths which have been delivered, ufeful to this whole Affembly, and by the confequent fruits may it appear, that in very deed God has been among us. And when we fhall feverally ftand in the great congregation of the affembled univerfe, by a precious holy life, may we be prepared to be found of our Judge in peace.

A M E N.